Pukeweed Soup

A New Tale to Tell
by
JoAnn Flammer

Lone Loon Press
Adirondack, New York, USA

To read is to learn, so read, read, read!

JoAnn Flammer

Pukeweed Soup
A New Tale to Tell

© 2013 by JoAnn Flammer

Visit the author at:
joannflammer.com
E-mail:
joannflammer@aol.com

ISBN-13:
978-0615789521 (Lone Loon Press)

ISBN-10:
0615789528

Lone Loon Press
Adirondack, New York

Printed in the United States

for
Brianna, Kristina, Andrew, Amber, & Alex
Grandchildren are the icing on the cake!

and for
Liz Cleveland and all her third graders patiently
waiting for this sequel-it was a long time coming.
Thank you for your encouragement and support.

With sincere appreciation to those who read my
manuscript for content and especially for
mechanics: Lee, Kathie, Sandi, Debbie, and Judi.

Chapter 1

Noah led his class into the auditorium. He walked along the row of seats and plopped down in the last seat. Willie settled in the seat next to him.

"Full house today," said Willie looking around the auditorium.

Noah's heart beat like a drum inside his chest. Soon the principal would introduce him and he would have to walk up onto the stage. He rubbed his clammy hands on his pant legs.

"You're going to ruin your new clothes," Willie said looking at Noah's neatly creased blue pants and pressed white shirt.

"Not new. Church clothes."

Noah looked at Willie dressed in jeans and his purple tee shirt with a bolt of lightning bold across his chest.

"Mom said I had to dress up." He wished he was in his jeans and tee shirt.

Willie leaned over close to Noah. "You're sweating there," whispered Willie pointing under Noah's nose.

"Ow," Noah muttered as Willie's spiked hair pricked his cheek. "Why don't you do something with that hair."

"I do. I wax it every morning," laughed Willie reaching up to pat the spikes. The short sleeve of his tee shirt pulled up to reveal a fire-breathing dragon tattoo. The colors were fading and the tail was peeling off.

"Your pet's disappearing," commented Noah. He wiped the sweat off his upper lip with his thumb.

Willie chuckled and pulled his other sleeve up to show off the new dragon wrapped around his left arm.

"Why are you so nervous?" asked Willie pulling both sleeves down.

"How would you like to go up there?" Noah exclaimed pointing to the stage at the front of the auditorium. Willie's great uncle, Willard, the Wise Wizard of Windom, stood next to the school principal. He looked impressive in his long flowing purple robe and pointy wizard hat.

Willie shuddered. As the Wee Wizard of Windom, he both respected and feared his powerful uncle.

"Chill. You'll do okay."

Noah heard his mom calling him. He looked over and waved. His dad gave him a thumbs up. Noah's stomach flip-flopped. He felt like throwing up. He spotted his sister, Ariel, and her friend, Belinda, jumping up and down. They were screaming his name, waving madly, with pony tails flapping behind them. He burrowed further into his seat.

"I think your sister wants you," Willie said.

"I know. I hear her," Noah muttered.

"Everyone hears her," Willie chuckled.

Noah turned and glared at Ari. She smiled at Noah, gave a final weak wave, and sat down.

Chapter 2

Squeaks and squeals came out of the mike. The principal tapped it, then blew into it.

"Please stand for the Pledge of Allegiance," he announced.

Everyone in the auditorium stood and faced the Stars and Stripes. With right hands over hearts, they recited the pledge and sat down.

Noah's heartbeat thundered in his ears.

"Go," said Willie poking Noah in the side.

"What?"

"Go!" Willie repeated.

"Come on down, Noah Banks," invited the principal.

Noah stood and ran his fingers through his short brown hair. He took a deep breath and started down the aisle.

The principal tapped the mike again. "While Noah's on his way up here, let me just say that we received many entries for Wizard Willard's creative writing contest. He informed me that the Council of Wizards enjoyed reading all of your solutions. However, only one story could be chosen to be acted out by the Theater Five Thespians. Each of you very inventive writers will receive a certificate of participation. Give yourselves a pat on the back. Good job, boys and girls."

Noah continued forward. He felt hundreds of eyes burning into his back as he stumbled past rows of students and tripped up the stage steps.

His face felt like it was on fire as he accepted the certificate and gift card to the local book store. He wiped his sweaty hand on his pants and shook

Uncle Willard's hand. The audience clapped and whistled.

As he mumbled his thanks, Noah thought, *I don't deserve this. I didn't make up a solution like everyone else did. My story really happened.* He had tried to tell everyone. But no one, not his mother or father or sister or friends, believed that Noah had been transported to Windom, saved his sister and solved Windom's dragon problem. They said he had been knocked out when he fell off of the slide in the park that day.

The white-bearded wizard smiled at Noah. He leaned forward and whispered into Noah's ear. "The people of Windom thank you for saving them from the dragon."

Noah's eyes widened.

"I have to talk to you," he whispered back.

"Soon," answered Uncle Willard. He winked at Noah. "We'll talk soon."

"Now we are proud to present *The Last Wish* by Noah Banks," announced the principal.

The audience continued to clap and cheer as Noah started down the steps. In the front row, Willie's brother, Reggie the Rhino, sat with his buddies. He twisted the end of his single spike of waxed black hair and pulled it forward to point out above his forehead like a rhinoceros horn. He snickered. He liked being called Reggie the Rhino.

Reggie poked the boys on either side of him.

"Let's make some noise," he said.

Together, they started to boo and heckle Noah.

Chapter 3

"Do you hear Reggie and his bully buddies?" growled Belinda.

"I hear them, Belly. They're being so mean," said Ari. Without thinking, she reached into her pocket. She pulled out a shiny gold coin, unconsciously rubbing it between her thumb and pointer.

"What's that?" asked Belly looking at the dragon stamped on the coin.

"This is the magic coin from Noah's story."

"Too bad it's not really magic."

"If only," Ariel whispered, glaring at Reggie the Rhino. "I'd wish…"

Something glittery to the right of the stage caught Noah's eye. He glanced over and spotted the gold coin he had thrown into the garbage months ago in his sister's hand. Ariel was glaring at Reggie as she rubbed the shiny coin between her thumb and pointer finger.

Oh, no, thought Noah. *Don't make a wish!*

A blue funnel of light sissed and flashed across the back of the stage.

The hair on the back of Noah's neck stood up.

He missed the last step and plunged forward, arms raised in the air.

Chapter 4

Willie had moved into Noah's empty seat. He clapped and gave a shrill whistle as Noah headed off the stage. He heard his brother Reggie and his buddies booing and heckling.

Willie saw Noah look toward Ari. He leaned into the aisle to see what Noah was looking at.

Ariel stood up, staring at Reggie. Something sparkled in her fingers. Willie leaned further out.

Oh, no. Is that Noah's magic coin she's rubbing?

Willie thought of the last time he'd seen that coin. He remembered the three-headed ostrich, the furbles, the fire-breathing dragon! Willie, the Wee Wizard of Windom, had reluctantly shared in Noah's Windom adventure. He didn't want a repeat. Willie leapt out of his seat and hurried down the aisle.

"No, Ari," he cried out, waving wildly. "Don't make a wish."

Willie spotted the blue light as it sissed and flashed across the back of the stage.

Everything changed to slow motion. Ari mouthing words as she made her wish. Reggie reaching out to block Noah's fall. Noah in mid-air, arms stretched over his head, diving for the hard auditorium floor.

But there was no hard floor for Noah. Instead, he dove into the middle of a huge blow-up mattress. He rolled softly into a double summersault and landed, stunned, sitting on the mattress, facing the stage.

Willie stood gaping open-mouthed at Noah as Ari, Belly, and Reggie reached his side.

"What the heck?!?!" cried Reggie the Rhino fists firm on his hips.

"Did you do that?" he asked his brother. "We're not allowed to use our powers yet. I'm telling …"

"No, uh, Ari…" Willie told Reggie pointing to the coin still clutched between her thumb and finger.

Belly held up Ari's hand. The gold coin twinkled like a shining star from the stage lights. "Ari did it," exclaimed Belly.

"Me?" Ari glanced from the coin to the mattress and back to the coin.

"Ariel?" Reggie shook his head. "That's my uncle's coin. Where'd you get it?" he asked.

"Who cares? She saved Noah's butt, didn't she?" Belly put her arm around her friend's shoulder.

"Wait," said Noah shaking the cobwebs out of his head. "You guys know about the magic coin?"

"Yes," answered Willie bowing his head. "The COW made us promise not to tell you."

Chapter 5

"What cow?" asked Ari.

"Cow's talk?" asked Belly.

Noah spun around on the mattress to face his sister and friends. His eyes grew wide. "What's with them?" he asked pointing to the audience.

Ariel, Belinda, Willie, and Reggie turned.

"No one's moving," said Noah.

"Or talking," said Reggie.

"Maybe not even breathing," agreed Willie.

"They're frozen!" exclaimed Ari.

Belly turned to the stage. "So are they," she added pointing to the principal and Uncle Willard.

"My uncle's frozen?" Willie asked.

"You can't freeze my uncle. He's a wizard. It's his coin. What did you do, Ari?" shouted Reggie the Rhino. He looked fierce with his head lowered and his spike of hair aimed at Ariel.

Tears formed in Ari's eyes. "I just wished Noah wouldn't get hurt."

"Well I didn't," stated Noah bouncing a little on the mattress. "Thanks, Ari."

"You're welcome."

"Now, how do we make everything go back to normal?" asked Noah looking at Willie and Reggie. "I'm guessing you guys are really wizards, right?"

"Yes, wizards-in-training, but we can't help," answered Willie. "The COW was so upset with us that it took away our wizard powers for a full year."

"Then the story was real?" questioned Ari. "Why don't I remember being…"

"Stop! How does a cow take away powers?" asked Belinda.

"Not a cow like in *animal*," explained Willie. "Short for Council of Wizards."

"You caused the problem, Ari," Reggie the Rhino said. "Just make another wish."

"No, you and your bully buddies caused the problem, Reggie, by booing and heckling Noah." Belly said. "Ari fixed it."

Ariel held up the coin.

"What should I say?"

"Say you're sorry and wish everything back," snarled Reggie.

Noah glared at Reggie while talking to Ariel. "You did right, Ari. Maybe you could just wish the mattress gone and the audience unfrozen."

"I wish the mattress gone and the audience unfrozen," said Ari.

Nothing happened.

"Try again and rub the coin at the same time," suggested Willie.

Ari rubbed the coin between her two fingers. "I wish the mattress gone and the audience un…"

"It was me. I *thought* the mattress so Noah would not get hurt," confessed a silvery voice from the stage.

Chapter 6

A girl stepped out from behind the frozen form of Uncle Willard.

Reggie's jaw dropped. He had never seen anyone as beautiful as this girl standing under the stage lights. Jewels sparkled from the gold crown that rested on her long, shiny brown hair. Her blue satin Cinderella gown stopped just above tiny white slippers. She glowed from head to toe!

She seemed to glide across the stage and down the steps.

Reggie the Rhino reached out to touch her. Her brown eyes widened and she stepped back.

"What are you doing?" Willie said pulling Reggie's arm back. "You're scaring her."

Reggie could not take his eyes off of the girl.

"She's … she's … wow!" he sputtered.

"Who are you?" asked Willie.

Noah stepped next to Willie.

"I am Princess Tai." She faced Noah. "And you are Noah. I need your help. You saved our villagers from the dragon. Please save our castle now."

"But … isn't the story fake?" Belly asked.

Ari looked at her brother. Noah shrugged his shoulders.

"I tried to tell everyone," he said. He looked at Reggie and then at Willie. They had been there when he saved the villagers, but now they seemed only interested in Princess Tai.

"Wait...wait...what do you mean you *thought* the mattress?" asked Willie. "How do you *think* a mattress?"

Tai touched the blue crystal hanging on the black ribbon around her neck. The crystal shone brightly at her touch.

"With this," she answered. "I *think* and it happens."

"Can I see?" asked Ari sidling up to Tai.

"Yes." Tai removed her hand and let Ari touch the crystal.

"It's not glowing anymore."

"No. It only works for me right now."

"Would you *think* something for us? Like ... like a puppy?" asked Belly leaning around Ari to touch the crystal. "I've always wanted a puppy."

"Or a million dollars," suggested Willie shaking his head. "I've always wanted a million dollars."

"Maybe she could just unfreeze everyone," said Ari.

"I don't even know *why* they are frozen," exclaimed Princes Tai.

"You're beautiful," Reggie told her. She smiled at Reggie.

"Cut it out, Reggie," said Willie. "Why don't you try," he told Tai.

Tai touched the crystal and it glowed blue.

"No. Stop. She's not *thinking* anything yet," said Noah.

"Noah is right. My mother gave it to me to come for Noah. I have not been trained yet to use it properly."

"Let's give Tai a chance to explain what this is about first."

Tai sighed. She took her hand off the crystal. "It is a very long story."

Princess Tai's Story

"My father is King Merek. We live in a castle in Windom."

Willie's eyes widened.

"Not Windom again," he moaned. He could almost feel the dragon's hot breath as the furbles had dragged him to its eating place.

An uneasy chill shivered up Reggie's spine. His Windom memories were not happy memories either.

"That's where your dragon story happened, isn't it, Noah?" Ari asked touching her brother's shoulder.

Noah nodded his head. "Go on," he said to Tai.

Tai smiled. "Yes, that is why I know about Noah. He is a hero in Windom. So here am I to get my castle saved…by Noah."

"Tell me it's not another dragon," begged Willie.

"So the dragon was real?" asked Ari.

She looked at each boy. All three nodded. Ari heaved a tremendous sigh. "I almost got eaten by a dragon. I'm glad I don't remember that."

"Wow!" exclaimed Belly.

"Why don't you start at the beginning, Tai," said Noah.

"OK. My father is king and his brother, my uncle, is the advisor. Recently, Father found an entrance to an old mine under the castle. They went into the tunnel and found diamonds. My uncle wants to start taking the diamonds from the mine, but my father says it is too dangerous digging so close to the castle. So, my uncle sent my father and all the soldiers from our kingdom on a wild duck chase."

"You mean wild goose chase," corrected Belly.

"Okay…wild goose chase. Then he called for his friend's army to come. They set up tents outside the castle. They put up wooden stands full of long rifles. No one can leave and no one can come in without the advisor's permission. He plans to capture my father and his men. They will have to fight when they return. They have no warning. Many may be killed.

"He has locked the women and girls in the dungeon and has the men and boys working in the mines. My mother, Queen Ellyn, hid me with her in the tunnel, but someone told on us. When we heard the advisor coming, Mother pushed me up onto a very high beam and gave me this crystal. She told me to go to get help from our hero, Noah. The advisor did not see me. I waited until they were gone then *thought* myself here, to Noah."

"Why didn't the queen just use the crystal to stop the advisor?" asked Willie hoping to get out of this new adventure.

"In the beginning, my mother tried to stop him but he is too powerful and he brought too many soldiers."

"I don't know what I could do to help, Tai," said Noah. "That whole dragon episode was just plain good luck. I wasn't brave. I had no choice about going because I had to get Ari back home. I was scared the whole time."

"But isn't that what bravery is? Saving someone even when you are scared?" asked Princess Tai.

"But I don't have any magic to wish us to Windom. And Willie and Reggie said they haven't gotten back their wizard rights. I'm really sorry, Tai, but I don't see how any of us can help you," stated Noah.

"Oh, I will *think* a wormhole to get us to Windom. Then you will find a way to help, maybe more *just plain good luck.* Please? Yes?" Her eyes filled with tears.

"I don't know ..." started Noah.

Reggie put a hand on Tai's shoulder. He looked into her big, brown, teary eyes. He sighed.

"Uh, why don't we ..." Reggie started.

Willy looked disgusted with his brother. "Reggie, think about it. What chance would we have against a big army and a powerful advisor?"

"But she needs me...uh, us," he sighed again as he watched the tear rolling down Tai's cheek. "I'll help you, Princess Tai," he declared.

"Thank you, Reggie."

"I'm in," said Ari reaching across Noah and gently touching Princess Tai's arm. "But I hope I remember this adventure."

"Me, too," echoed Belly.

"No way are you going, Ari, or you either, Belly," stated Noah. "All right, Princess. I'll come and see if I can help. How about you, Willie? Are you with Reggie and me?"

"I don't know. I mean last time …" he said reluctantly. Noah and Reggie glared at him. "Okay, okay. I'll go," he said.

"I'm going. You're not the boss of me, Noah," pouted Ari. "Belly and I want to go."

Belinda nodded. "Princess Tai must need us or we would have been frozen like everyone else in this auditorium. Even Uncle Willard, the Wise Wizard of Windom, is frozen."

"Hey, she's right. Why is my uncle frozen? Couldn't he help?" asked Willie still looking for a way out.

"Yeah! Unfreeze him," agreed Reggie, "so he can come with us. My uncle is probably more powerful than your uncle."

Tai looked at Uncle Willard standing like a statue on the stage. She was confused. Why was he frozen and the girls not? She touched the crystal hanging on the black ribbon around her neck and tried to unfreeze Uncle Willard, but nothing happened. She wished she knew more about using her mother's precious crystal.

"I fear that Ariel is right. I did not select anyone here but Noah, yet Willie, Reggie and the girls are not frozen. It is final. The blue crystal has decided who will come to Windom."

Chapter 8

Tai reached for her necklace.

"Touch her everyone," said Belly, "before she *thinks* Windom."

"With pleasure," murmured Reggie putting his arm around Tai's shoulder.

"That's not necessary," she said smiling at Reggie.

Reluctantly, he removed his arm.

As her palm closed around the crystal, a flash of blue light sissed and streaked in front of the stage. A small, black hole opened up behind her.

"This will take us to Windom," she said.

"It's too small for all of us," said Reggie concerned that he would not be able to follow Tai to Windom.

"Don't worry. It will change to fit each of us."
Ari laughed. "It's a one-size-fits-all wormhole."

Belly giggled. Reggie chuckled. Noah smiled.

"Go ahead, make jokes. This is just plain crazy," said Willie. "We have no idea what we're getting ourselves into."

Tai put her hand on Willie's arm. "Noah will save us. I know he will," she whispered to Willie.

"I'm not so sure," he mumbled.

"Follow me," Tai told the group. "When you come out in the tunnel, quickly hide behind something until we are all there."

"Wait, what?" cried Willie as Tai turned and entered the wormhole. "Hide … hide from what?"

The princess was swallowed up instantly.

Reggie leaped in after Tai.

Ari grabbed Belly's hand and they jumped into the black hole together.

Willie looked at Noah.

"I don't know…Princess Tai said hide…but from…" he started.

Noah rolled his eyes. He pushed Willie in, then jumped in himself.

Chapter 9

Princess Tai tumbled out of the wormhole onto the hard packed dirt of the tunnel floor. She landed with a thud between the tracks that carried carts full of rock and dirt out of the tunnel. The lights hanging from the tunnel walls were dim but she could still see the red coats of the soldiers. They were guarding men and boys her uncle had sent down to mine diamonds. The workers were covered in dust from hammering at the rock with pickaxes. Tai scooted behind a nearby cart and waited for the others to come through.

Reggie slammed into the tunnel wall and fell behind the cart at Tai's feet. He was dizzy and his eyes crossed when he looked at her.

"Whoa" he said standing and balancing himself. "There's two of you."

"Shh, Reggie. Get down here next to me," she whispered pulling Reggie low behind the cart.

"With pleasure," he said crouching as close as he could to Tai.

"You got dirt all over your gown," he said. "Not the best outfit for tunnels."

"You are right. Maybe I can trade clothes."

"With me?" squeaked Reggie.

Tai laughed. "No, with this." She touched the blue crystal. Her princess clothes became jeans and a tee shirt.

"Ah, that's better," said Reggie.

Ari and Belly arrived together in a flurry of arms and legs in the middle of the tunnel.

"Dizzzzzzzy," Belly said raising up from her knees. Ari spotted Tai and Reggie behind the cart. Tai pointed to the soldiers. Ari grabbed Belly's hand and they took cover behind a big straw basket. Ari lifted the lid. It was empty.

"Quick. In here," she encouraged Belly. The girls climbed into the basket and pulled the lid over themselves. Ari peeked out and Tai gave her a thumbs up.

"Where's your pretty gown?" asked Ari.

"These are better for saving a castle," answered Tai.

"What's taking Noah and Willie so long?" Reggie asked.

"They will come," Tai answered.

Willie rolled out of the wormhole with Noah right on his heels.

"Crazy ride," Noah mumbled. He looked at Willie holding his stomach.

"You're white as a ghost," Noah said.

Willie stood up, bent over, and threw up.

"Ugh. This is like déjà vu, only this time it's you throwing up, " said Noah remembering his last trip to Windom. He moved out of Willie's way.

"Sorry," moaned Willie holding his stomach.

Noah caught site of Tai and Reggie. He looked around worriedly.

"Where's Ari?" he whispered.

"Here," Ari hissed waving her hand outside the lid. "We're in here."

Noah sighed in relief. "Okay. What now?"

"Hey, who are you?" shouted one of the soldiers. "What are you guys doing over there?" He started down the tunnel toward Noah and Willie.

"Run! We must get to the kitchen," yelled Tai.

The girls jumped out of the basket. They followed Tai and Reggie through the tunnel. Willie tripped. Noah helped him up.

"Go," Noah shouted pushing him after the group.

Noah stopped by the basket.

Willie started to follow the others. He looked back at Noah.

"What are you doing?" Willie cried.

"Slowing him down," Noah said.

Noah grabbed the basket the girls had been in and pushed it into the middle of the tunnel. Then he tried to turn the cart over. It was too heavy for him.

Willie moaned. He raced back.

"Quick. Let's do it together," he told Noah.

The boys got on one side and shoved until the heavy metal cart flipped onto its side blocking the tunnel. They ran down to the next cart and did the same thing.

"What's this?" said Willie bending to pull at a piece of black ribbon sticking out from under the cart.

The soldier cried out. Willie let go of the ribbon and looked up just in time to see the soldier slip and slide along the tunnel floor into the basket.

"I guess he found my throw-up."

"Lucky for us," Noah said. "Let's catch up to Tai and the gang."

"Where did they go?" asked Willie.

"We'll find them. They'll wait for us somewhere."

Chapter 10

Tai reached a gray metal door at the end of the tunnel. She bent over with her hands on her knees and took a few deep breaths.

"You okay?" Reggie asked.

"Yes, just winded."

Ari and Belly caught up huffing and puffing. Tai shushed them with a finger over her lips, then slowly pulled the heavy door just a few inches toward her. She peaked into the crack.

"No one there. Come on," Tai said.

"Where's Noah?" asked Ari. "We have to wait for Noah."

"He will find us…there's no place else to go."

Ari put her arm through Belly's and stepped through the door into a well-lit stairwell. They started up the stairs after Tai and Reggie.

"Where does this go?" called Ari.

"To the kitchens. We must be very quiet. It is a long time since breakfast, but there might be someone there preparing lunch."

They reached the top of the stairs and faced another gray metal door. A sign said Soldiers' Quarters.

"Not this level," said Tai. "We must go up to the very top, the door to the kitchen." They turned and started up the next flight of steps.

"Where does the next door go?" asked Reggie.

"Outside to the courtyard…where the army is camped. We don't want to go there."

"No, we don't," said Ari and Belly at the exact same time.

"Jinx," called Belly connecting her pinkie finger to Ari's. "You owe me a coke." Ari put her hand over Belly's mouth and the two girls giggled nervously.

"What is that 'owe me a coke?'" whispered Tai.

"When two people say the same thing, the first one to call 'jinx' gets treated to something by the other person. It's stupid kid stuff," Reggie told Tai.

Ari and Belly rolled their eyes at Reggie.

When the group reached the courtyard door, Tai put her hand up to stop them. She leaned against the door and listened. Reggie put his head against the door nose to nose with Tai.

"What are we listening for?" he asked.

"Soldiers. They are right outside. I hear them talking."

Reggie stepped away from the door, eyes wide.

"Let's go," he said pulling Tai away from the door. "We don't want to get caught by any soldiers working for your uncle."

He started up the next set of stairs pushing Tai ahead of him.

Ari and Belly scooted up behind them.

The last door had a big sign on it that said Kitchen Staff Only. Tai held up her hand again and the group stopped.

"There should not be anyone in there at this time, but just in case, let me go in alone. If it is safe, I will come and get you."

"Wait," said Reggie holding Tai's arm. "What do we do if you don't come out for us?"

"Let her go," said Ari. "We don't have much of a choice."

Reggie released Tai's arm.

"I don't like this," he murmured. "What if she gets captured and put in the dungeon?"

"She can use her blue think crystal," said Belly.

Princess Tai reached to feel the safety of the crystal.

"It's gone!" she exclaimed. "It must have fallen off back in the tunnel. Mother will be so upset," Tai said.

"We can't worry about that now," said Ari.

Princess Tai nodded. She put her ear to the cold metal of the door. Then she pushed in slowly and peeked around the edge.

"It looks empty," she whispered. "I will check quickly."

Tai disappeared inside the kitchen. Reggie held the heavy door slightly ajar. He tapped his foot on the landing.

"Stop tapping your foot like that," said Belly. "You'll get us caught."

"She's taking too long," he answered.

Reggie pushed the door in just as Tai pulled it open.

"It is safe," she said.

The group moved into the kitchen and the door closed with a soft click.

Chapter 11

Noah reached the door at the end of the tunnel first. He pulled it open and stepped into the stairwell. The soft click of a door closing sounded above.

Willie skidded into Noah.

"Humpf. Hey, take it easy," warned Noah holding the door frame to keep himself from falling.

"Where is everyone?" whispered Willie.

"I just heard a door close up there."

"Was it Princess Tai and the others?"

"Don't know." Noah tiptoed further into the stairwell and looked up. "Don't see anyone. There's no place to go but up."

"Wait," said Willie holding the door to the tunnel open. "How do we know…"

An alarm sounded. Red lights flashed in the tunnel.

"That soldier must have set off the alarm," said Noah.

Willie looked back and saw not one, but two, soldiers heading toward them. He let the door close and joined Noah in the stairwell. The boys raced up the stairs. They stopped at the first landing.

"Soldiers' Quarters. This isn't it," said Noah. "Tai said something about a kitchen." They raced up the next flight of stairs.

One of the soldiers chasing them opened the tunnel door and entered the stairwell. At the same time, the door to the soldiers' quarters opened and a man dressed in uniform pants and a tee shirt stepped onto the landing.

"What's going on?" he called down.

"Some kids trying to escape," the soldier answered pointing up.

The staircase shook as three soldiers pounded up the steps after them.

Noah and Willie reached the door labeled 'Courtyard.'

"It's not the kitchen, but we have to get out of this stairwell now."

Willie pointed to a small, square box with numbers next to the door.

"We need a security code."

"No time to play with numbers," said Noah.

He pushed on the bar across the door and set off a new set of alarms.

"This is not going well," moaned Willie.

Noah grabbed his arm and pulled him outside. They stumbled as the bright sun blinded them.

"Can't see," said Willie tripping and waving his arms in the air for balance.

"You'll be okay in a second."

Noah spotted a wood container with a lid to the right of the building.

"Got to be a composting bin," he said.

He dragged a bumbling Willie along.

"Get in," Noah ordered.

"It smells," complained Willie.

"Some smells save lives," quoted Noah remembering last week's fire safety lesson.

"Yes, but I don't think they meant these smells," answered Willie holding his nose.

Noah boosted Willie into the decaying plant matter and dove in after him.

Chapter 12

Screeching sirens echoed off the kitchen walls.

"Oh, no," cried Ari. "We've got to help Noah and Willie." She turned to open the big gray door.

Reggie pulled her away from the door. "You're going to get us all caught! What good would that do them?"

"He's right," said Princess Tai. "We don't even know if they have been taken."

Reggie released Ari's arm. His heart swelled with pride. Tai said he was right. He moved next to Tai and stood a little taller.

"What should we do now, Princess?" he asked.

"We have to come up with a way to keep my uncle's army from attacking my father and his men when they return."

"We can't stop a whole army," Belly groaned.

"I wish you had your crystal," said Ari.

"The coin! Maybe it will work here," stated Belly.

Ari checked her pockets. "It's not here. I think I dropped it back in the auditorium when I saw Princess Tai."

"How about getting to your father and warning him about the army?" suggested Reggie.

"We sent someone to find and warn Father twice. Both times they were caught by the soldiers and put back in the mine."

A new alarm sounded and Tai walked to the window.

"That is the alarm for the courtyard door. Someone has gone outside without putting in the security code."

The girls hurried to the window.

"There's a million soldiers out there," cried Belly. At least a dozen white tents dotted the hillside. Sunlight sparkled off rifles standing in wood racks beside each tent. Soldiers in red uniforms shot at targets in the field across the moat surrounding the castle. A small group marched across the bridge in time to a drummer. A handful of soldiers sat at a table outside the tents playing cards.

"I don't think it's a million, but there sure are a lot of red coats," said Ari.

"Look," pointed Reggie.

They watched as Noah disappeared into the compost bin.

The sound of the alarms had soldiers grabbing rifles and running across the drawbridge. More soldiers came from the castle and met them. A soldier on horseback galloped to their side.

"What do you think they're saying?" asked Belly.

"I don't know, but they must not have seen Noah and Willie," said Tai. "They are safe…for now."

The soldier on horseback pointed at the castle and the men with him looked up.

"Duck down," cried Reggie pushing on Ari's and Belly's heads.

"Hey," cried the girls in unison. A nervous giggle erupted and they clasped pinkies again. "Jinx," said Belly.

Reggie rolled his eyes.

Tai moved to the side of the window.

"The girls are just releasing some stress," she said smiling at Reggie.

Reggie's heart actually skipped a beat. *I'm in love*, he thought smiling back.

Tai peeked out the window. She spotted her uncle leaning out a nearby window shouting orders down to the soldiers.

"The advisor is talking to them," said Tai. She pushed the window open a tiny bit.

"Find them," he shouted down to the soldiers.

Chapter 13

Tai looked at the clock above the swinging door that opened into the dining room.

"Kitchen workers will be coming in to prepare lunch soon. We must find a place to …"

The door swung in and a huge bear of a man in a white apron entered the kitchen. A tall, white chef's hat covered his head.

Ariel, Belinda, and Reggie froze.

The man lifted up his arms and Tai ran to him.

"What are you wearing, child?" he asked raising his bushy eyebrows.

Princess Tai laughed. "Clothes for saving our castle."

She stretched her arms around his big belly.

"Domi, you are freed. Mother, too?" she queried leaning back to look into his warm, brown eyes.

"No, child," he said sadly. "I am freed only to work the kitchen this day."

"Why, what happened to my uncle's new cook?"

"One of his young kitchen helpers accidentally picked lobelia from the garden and crushed a leaf into the breakfast for the kitchen staff," laughed Domi. "They are still very sick to their stomachs and want only to lay down all day."

"Oh, lucky for us," smiled Tai. She turned to her new friends. "This is Domi. He is like an uncle to me," she said laying her head against his massive chest.

"What is lobelia?" asked Ari.

"It is a plant from the king's garden that is used as a medicine. Some must have grown in with the herbs and spices by accident. The helper didn't recognize it," answered Domi.

"It's to make you throw up if you eat poison or something. It's also called pukeweed," said Tai.

"Sounds yucky," said Belly.

"Yes. It is," agreed Domi. "So, is this the hero, Noah, your mother said you might bring here?" Domi asked putting his arm around Reggie's shoulder.

"No, he is not Noah," said Tai sadly.

Reggie frowned. His cheeks turned pink. "The big *hero* is outside *hiding* in the compost bin with my brother."

"They are hiding from the soldiers," defended Ari.

"So that is the reason for all the alarms?" asked Domi.

"Yes."

Tai finished introducing Reggie and the girls to Domi.

Domi patted Reggie on the back. He smiled at the girls.

"They will be our new heroes then, yes?"

Reggie stood taller. He smiled and nodded.

"We will do our best," he said.

Chapter 14

Footsteps echoed in the stairwell. The big gray door pushed in. Domi shoved Princess Tai behind him just as two soldiers burst into the room.

"What is this?" bellowed the taller one, pistol pointed at Domi. "Where is Gargo?"

Domi put his hands up. Tai stayed as still as a statue behind Domi. Reggie and the girls were glued to their spots.

"It's alright. Gargo is sick," said the second soldier. He pointed to Domi. "He is cooking today." The soldier lowered his gun.

Domi pointed to the door under the cabinet by the sink.

"Put on your aprons," he instructed the children. Ari reached under the sink and pulled out three aprons.

"These are my helpers," Domi told the soldiers.

Ari handed the aprons to Reggie and Belly. They put them on and started moving around the kitchen.

"He is big and strong," said the smaller soldier pointing to Reggie. "He should be working below in the mines."

Reggie paled. He looked at Domi.

"I need him here. The girls are scrawny and weak. He must lift and carry."

Ari made a face at Domi. Belly rolled her eyes. The soldiers laughed.

"Well, be careful. Some mine workers have escaped. We chased them into the stairwell," said the taller soldier.

"We will find them, punish them, then put them back to work in the underground mines."

Ari shivered. Belly hugged her arms around her waist. Reggie's face grew even paler.

The soldiers turned and marched out.

Tai came out from behind Domi.

"Thank you. They would have recognized me and locked me up." She hugged Domi.

Everyone breathed a sigh of relief.

Chapter 15

Noah removed a piece of wet lettuce from his ear and listened against the side of the compost bin. He could hear men talking. They sounded very close. He lifted the lid just a hair and peeked out. Red coats with black leather belts blocked his view.

Willie reached across Noah to lift the lid up higher so he could see. Willie lost his balance and fell forward accidentally pushing Noah's hand away. The lid dropped with a *boing*. The container jiggled.

"What was that?" asked one of the soldiers standing next to the compost bin.

"It sounded like it was right behind us," replied his companion.

They turned and faced the container.

Inside, Noah and Willie covered themselves with rotted vegetables and other kitchen scraps.

"Be prepared to jump out and run," whispered Noah. Willie, holding his nose, nodded his agreement.

"It must have been from inside there," stated the first soldier.

"There's probably a furble or a raccoon inside. Let's leave it be."

The soldiers started walking away.

The big steel door opened and Reggie in his white helper's apron trotted out carrying a bucket of scraps from the kitchen. Ari & Belly held the heavy door open.

Reggie spotted the soldiers and stopped.

"Better be careful dumping that," a soldier called to him. He pointed to the compost bin. "We just heard some noises coming from inside."

Reggie lowered his eyes. He moved to the container and put the pail down.

"Ok. Thanks," he called back.

The soldiers watched as Reggie lifted the lid. Nothing came scurrying out.

"It must have escaped." The soldiers continued on their way.

Reggie picked up the pail. He started dumping it slowly.

"You guys in here?" he murmured.

"Yeah," said Noah.

"Quit dumping more stuff on us," Willie wailed.

"There are two aprons in the bottom of this pail. Put them on. I'll tell you when to come out."

"Phew. This stinks worse than the the stuff rotting in here," complained Willie pulling an apron over his head.

"Uh, duh. Were you hoping for sweet smelling compost?" said Reggie snickering.

The boys put the apron bibs over their heads and pulled the strings around back, tying them in the front.

"Maybe we should wait until dark," Willie suggested.

"No. Domi says the stuff in here gets turned with a pitchfork soon."

"Who is Domi?" Noah asked.

"We'll explain when you're safe," said Reggie.

Reggie shook the pail. Then he banged it against the edge as he looked around. There were soldiers on the bridge and across the moat. No one was looking his way.

"Now," he told Noah and Willie.

The two boys climbed out of the compost bin and stood next to Reggie. They wiped food and scraps out of their hair and shook it off their bodies.

"What now?" Noah asked Reggie.

"Quick. Get inside the castle."

The three boys trotted to the door. Ari & Belly held it wide.

When they were inside, Ari hugged her brother. Belly patted his arm.

"You smell," Ari said. Noah grinned.

"It's good to see you, too."

"Let's hurry upstairs," she said.

"Why didn't the alarm go off when you opened the door?" Willie asked starting up the stairs next to Belly.

"Domi gave us the security code," answered Reggie giving his brother a smack on the back of his head with the palm of his hand.

"You missed me, didn't you?" Willie reached around Belly to smack Reggie back.

Reggie leaned back and caught Willie's wrist. Belly got stuck in the middle.

"Hey," she cried when Willie almost knocked her off the step.

"OK, guys. Cut it out," said Noah. "So who is this Domi?" he asked.

"I am Domi," came the booming voice of the big, bald man who opened the door to the kitchen. "And you are too noisy."

Princess Tai stood next to him smiling.

Pukeweed Soup

"We have to think now," said Domi as everyone gathered in the kitchen. His tall, white chef's hat sat on the long wooden table in the center of the kitchen.

"Princess Tai's father and his men are expected back this evening from their wild duck chase."

"Goose," corrected Belly.

"Goose?" queried Domi.

"Goose chase, not duck chase," explained Ari.

"Anyway, they will not be prepared for this battle. We must make a plan," said Domi.

"Plan what?" whined Willie. "Plan how? We're just kids. Those soldiers have guns and they shoot to kill." Willie wished this was a dream. A very bad dream.

"Exactly," answered Domi. "So, how do we stop them from shooting the king and his soldiers?"

"Take away their guns?" asked Belly shrugging her shoulders and raising her hands in the air.

"Fat chance," said Reggie standing next to Tai. He looked to see if she agreed.

"You are right, Reggie. They will not give up their guns easily."

Reggie smiled and nodded at Tai. He liked when she agreed with him. It made him feel like a prince…or even a king.

"Maybe we can distract them somehow," suggested Noah. "Then when they are distracted, we go get their rifles off the wood racks."

"Good idea. If you have any fireworks…" started Belly.

"No, that would only make them grab their rifles," said Domi.

"Even if we did find a way to distract them, who's going for the guns?" asked Willie. "There's just too many of them and not enough of us."

"How about we send them on their own wild duck … I mean goose chase?" suggested Princess Tai.

"No, the advisor will not let his army leave so fast," said Domi.

"Or," said Ari with a wide grin on her face. "Maybe we can make them sick."

"Oh, yeah. Let's give them the flu," mocked Willie."We can go sneeze all over them."

Noah glared at him.

"This is serious," scolded Tai.

"Wait," said Domi. "The young lady may have something. What are you thinking, Ariel?"

"Lobelia. You know. Pukeweed."

Everyone looked at Ari.

"What are you talking about?" asked Noah.

"She means the plant that made all the kitchen helpers sick. Right, Ari?" asked Belly.

"Yes. Domi says it's right outside in the king's garden."

"Why does the king grow throw up weed?" asked Willie.

"It's pukeweed and it's medicine to make you throw up if you eat poison or something bad," Ari explained.

"One of the kitchen workers accidentally put it in the kitchen staff's food this morning. Everyone in the kitchen got sick. That is why they had to free Domi from the mines to come up and cook for today," continued Tai.

"Soldiers with cramps and diarrhea and vomiting…Ari, I think you will be our new hero," said Domi.

Chapter 17

Noah punched in the security code. He carried the basket that Ari would fill with pukeweed. Reggie was right behind them carrying the two baskets for Belly and Willie to fill with fresh vegetables. Once outside, they turned right and walked along the side of the castle. Willie shuddered as they passed the compost bin that had been his temporary refuge.

"Phew," jeered Reggie. "Smells just like you, brother." He slapped Willie on the back of the head.

Willie reached to slap Reggie back. Reggie side-stepped to avoid the hit and smacked the back of his brother's head again. Willie jumped on Reggie's back. Reggie started swatting him and yelling, "Get off of me!"

"Hey, you kids. Where are you going?" shouted a red-coated soldier standing by the bridge over the moat.

Reggie shrugged Willie off his back.

Noah turned around and spotted the three soldiers playing cards looking their way. He started walking backward.

"Uh, we're going to the garden…uh, to pick vegetables for your lunch," he yelled.

"Well quit horsing around and get to it or I'll send you down to the mines to work." The soldiers laughed as the five children started jogging toward the garden.

"You two better quit fooling around," lectured Belly huffing and puffing. "You almost got us caught."

"Sorry," said Willie hurrying past Noah and the girls. "Let's just get this done so we can get back in the kitchen. I don't like all these soldiers out here."

"Me either," added Reggie pushing his way
ahead of Willie.

Chapter 18

In the king's garden, Noah and Ari walked to the section separated by the sign with a red cross on a white background. When she found the lobelia plant, Ari carefully clipped off small sprigs and put them in the basket Noah carried.

Reggie placed his two baskets at the end of the rows of vegetables. Then he and the girls walked along pulling up carrots and onions, and picking tomatoes, celery and parsley.

When the baskets were filled, the children scurried back to the kitchen. Reggie dumped his two baskets into one of the double sinks under the window.

"You three girls start washing then cutting up those vegetables," directed Domi.

He pointed to the second sink. "Dump the lobelia in there, Noah. I'll wash and chop the leaves into really tiny pieces. We have to be careful not to put too much in. We only need the soldiers out of the picture until the king and his men arrest them. Ari, you'd better scrub your hands in the sink over there so you don't get sick from picking pukeweed."

Noah collected the empty baskets and put them back on the shelf. "What else can I do?" he asked.

"Grab two of those giant pots and start filling them with water. They will be heavy. Get Reggie and Willie to help you."

Ari started chopping carrots next to Princess Tai and Belly. "I sure hope this works," Ari mumbled to her best friend.

"Me, too," answered Belly. Tai nodded.

An hour later, two big pots of pukeweed soup simmered on the stove and the kitchen was once again spotless.

"What now?" asked Willie.

"We wait," answered Domi pulling a deck of cards out of a drawer under the long wooden table in the middle of the room.

"Go Fish anyone?"

Chapter 19

GONG! GONG! GONG!

The dining room filled quickly with hungry soldiers. The boys carried heavy tureens of soup and placed them in the center of the tables for the men to help themselves. Ari and Belly carried in the baskets of rolls and butter. Domi stood watching by the kitchen door. Tai stayed hidden in the kitchen.

A soldier with gold braid on his uniform and hat entered. He glared at Domi and shouted across the room, "Who are you? Where is our cook?"

"I am Domi, Captain. Your cook is ill. I was put in charge."

"Do not eat," he instructed his men. They put down their spoons.

"You," he said pointing to Domi, "must eat first."

Willie gasped. Noah poked him into silence. Ari and Belly exchanged worried glances. Reggie mumbled, "He'll get sick."

Domi walked to the nearest table. He smiled at the captain. Then he dipped a cup into the tureen and swallowed a big gulp of soup. He sputtered.

"Ah. It's hot," he told the soldiers, "so be careful not to burn yourselves."

The captain nodded his approval. "The cook has eaten. It is safe. Dig in," he told the hungry soldiers. "The king's army is close. They will be here in a couple of hours."

"They're wolfing down this stuff so fast," said Noah filling another tureen with the pukeweed soup.

"Noah, my father needs to know what is happening here. Someone has to warn him," whispered Tai from her hiding place behind the door. "They must know what they are riding into."

"But how?" asked Noah.

"Can you ride a horse bareback?" she asked.

"You mean without a saddle?"

"Yes. My uncle has removed all the saddles from the stable to stop us from getting to my father."

Noah thought. "I'm a good rider. I think I can do it."

"My horse is in the stable. He is a brown and white pinto."

"What are you two talking about?" asked Willie setting down another tureen to refill.

"I'm going to warn Tai's dad," answered Noah.

"By horse?" asked Willie.

"I'll go to the stables while the soldiers are busy eating," said Noah.

"That sounds too dangerous. Why not just *think* him to your father?"

"I lost my crystal," answered Princess Tai touching the empty spot by her neck.

Willie smacked his forehead.

"That was the black ribbon I saw under the cart in the tunnel," he exclaimed.

"What did you see in the tunnel?" asked Belly carrying an empty bread basket.

"Willie saw a piece of…never mind. There's no time for that now. I've got to warn King Merek," said Noah.

Chapter 20

Noah entered the security code and stepped out into the bright sunshine. As his eyes adjusted, he carried the slop pail from the kitchen to the compost bin. He opened the lid and dumped the scraps. He looked around. No one seemed to be watching him, so he walked slowly toward the stable.

"Hey, where are you going, kid?" A soldier turned from the bridge and headed in his direction.

"To the stable … uh, to make sure the horses have water," answered Noah still walking to the stable.

Another soldier opened the door to the courtyard. He leaned out.

"Sarge, you better get in here to eat or there won't be anything left," he called.

"On my way," he said turning away from Noah.

Noah hurried the rest of the way to the stable. He unlatched the half-door to Tai's horse's stall and walked the pinto into the yard. He looked toward the woods and saw the path Princess Tai told him to take. Then he grabbed a hank of the horse's mane, pulled himself up, and galloped off to find the king.

Chapter 21

Domi finished ladling soup into another tureen and carried it to the wall next to the bulletin board.

"What are you doing?" asked Ariel.

"We have to get this soup to the men in the dungeon and tunnels."

Princess Tai walked over to Domi and opened a small door in the middle of the wall.

"What's that?" Reggie asked moving to Tai's side.

"It's called a dumbwaiter. I put the food here, pull this rope, and the food goes below."

"Kind of like a little elevator," said Ari.

"It saves the kitchen servers from having to go up and down the three flights of stairs."

"Wow," said Belinda. "That's cool."

Domi lowered the soup tureen to the shelf. He pulled the rope slowly to send the cart through the shaft to the dungeon. Tai pulled another rope and the children could hear the sound of a bell ringing below to tell the soldiers their food had arrived.

"Ha! Not so dumb," exclaimed Reggie.

Domi and the children went back into the dining room. They cleared and washed the tables.

"Domi, I am sorry you had to eat some soup." Princess Tai hugged her friend's arm.

"Yes, you were so brave." Ari patted him on the back. "Thank you."

"I hope you don't get too sick," said Belly.

"I will be fine. I did not eat much." Domi's belly grumbled loudly.

"Hey, why isn't Noah in here cleaning up this mess with us?" asked Reggie.

"He's busy somewhere else," said Willie.

"Well, it's not fair ..." Willie poked his brother in the ribs.

"Cut that out," complained Reggie.

"Yes, where is my brother?" asked Ariel looking around.

Willie shuffled back and forth. "Uh, he's gone to warn Tai's dad."

Domi stopped. He put down the heavy tray of dishes.

"Princess. What have you done?" he asked Tai.

"Noah has gone to warn my father of the danger here," she sighed. "I thought with soldiers eating, it would be a good time."

"Oh, no." Ari buried her face in her hands.

"He made it safely to the stable. I watched him ride off into the trees," said Willie patting Ari's back.

"He'll be all right," encouraged Belly standing beside her friend.

"Let us hope this ends soon," said Domi shaking his head.

Chapter 22

As they put away the last of the washed and dried dishes, pots, pans and utensils, they heard another rumble in Domi's stomach.

"Uh, oh," he said. "It's about to start." Domi hurried from the room holding his stomach.

"What's about to start?" asked Willie.

"Uh, duh. The pukeweed. It's going to start working on the soldiers, too," said Reggie.

Everyone rushed to the windows above the sink.

They watched men in red coats rush to the outhouses only to find long lines waiting to get in. Others, bent over, holding their stomachs, scurried into the trees behind the white tents to throw up. Some dragged themselves into their tents, standing their rifles in the wood racks. They did not come back out.

"Rifles," said Ari. "We have to get all their guns."

"How?" Belly asked.

"While they are sick, we can take them and throw them in the water that sits in the moat under the bridge," said Princess Tai heading toward the stairs.

"There's way too many for us," said Reggie holding her back.

"Then let's free everyone in the dungeon and the mines," suggested Ari.

"Again, how?" asked Belly.

Ari walked to the dumbwaiter. She opened the door and heard the moans of soldiers echoing in the shaft.

"They're sick, too. I'll go down in the dumbwaiter and free everyone." Ari began pulling the cart up with the rope.

"No, I'll go down. I can fight the sick soldiers if I have to." Reggie made a fist and flexed the muscles in his arm.

"No," said Willie. "I'm smaller than you. I'll go. We need your strength to let the rope down slowly until it reaches the bottom. And no fooling around."

"I'll get you down there safely, brother," said Reggie earnestly.

"You are all so brave," said Tai. Reggie flexed his muscles one again and preened like a peacock.

Chapter 23

When the dumbwaiter hit bottom, Willie crawled out onto the damp stone floor. Two soldiers lay doubled over, holding their bellies, moaning. Willie held his nose as he stepped around their twisted bodies.

"Phew," he mumbled. "You guys smell worse than the compost bin."

He grabbed the keys off the wall and raced to unlock the cells.

"Who are you?" asked a lovely lady who looked just like Princess Tai.

"No time to explain," said Willie opening the cell doors and releasing all the women and children.

"Follow me. Princess Tai needs everyone's help to throw all the rifles under the bridge."

As they passed the mine entrance, Willie saw soldiers squirming like worms on the dirt floor of the mine. He shouted to the men and boys to follow him. Everyone followed Willie through the tunnel and up the stairs.

Reggie, Ariel, and Belinda were just coming down. They all met at the door that opened onto the courtyard. The lady who had questioned Willie grabbed Princess Tai and hugged her.

"Mama," cried Princess Tai.

"Thank God, you are safe!"

"We need to …"

"Yes, this young man told us," Queen Ellyn said.

She entered the security code for the door. Men, women, and children raced across the bridge and began grabbing rifles to throw into the water.

Soldiers' moans and groans filled the air as they moved in and out of tents. No one stopped them from grabbing rifles off the wood racks and dumping them into the moat.

"Look, there," cried Ariel pointing toward the field. "It's Noah."

Noah lay across the back of the brown and white pinto holding tight to the galloping horse's mane. Next to him, the king sat atop a pure white stallion, tearing across the field toward the tents. His army charged behind them.

A horse and rider sprinted out of the nearby stable.

"It's my uncle…he's getting away," yelled Tai pointing to a black-caped man galloping out of the stable.

The king raced after him. He knocked the advisor off of his horse. They struggled on the ground for a few minutes, but the advisor was not as strong as his brother. King Merek pushed him toward the group standing by the bridge.

The soldiers from the advisor's army had all been gathered together on the practice field. The king's men, still on horseback, circled the men who had been drained and weakened by the pukeweed soup. The advisor knew it was all over for him.

Chapter 24

Domi came running out of the castle buckling his pants.

"You have defeated the advisor," he exclaimed.

"Are you okay?" cried Princess Tai and Belly in unison.

"Jinx," Belly and Tai exclaimed hooking pinkies.

"You owe me a coke," said Belinda.

"I think I owe you a lot more than a coke," laughed Tai.

Turning to Domi she said, "You have recovered?"

"I am fine. The sickness does not last long," Domi said.

King Merek stepped forward.

"What happened here? Who are these children? And where are your clothes?" he asked the princess.

"This is partly my doing," said Queen Ellyn. She explained about the advisor's army and giving Tai the blue crystal.

Princess Tai took over the story relating how her new friends had come to help. She explained that her jeans and tee shirt were more suited to saving a kingdom.

Domi told his part in how he became the cook for today and how Ari suggested making pukeweed soup for the soldiers.

King Merek stood with his hands behind his back, rocking back and forth in his black boots.

"That is quite a tale. I cannot believe he tricked me with his wild duck chase."

"Goose," five voices chanted in unison. They laughed.

"What is goose?" asked the queen not understanding the laughter.

"Much like our wild ducks I suspect," answered her husband. Turning to the children he said, "There is no such thing as a goose in Windom."

"That explains that," laughed Noah.

"Well, we are certainly in your debt," King Merek said bowing to the children.

"Glad we could help," said Noah. "But it's really Ari who saved the day."

"Yes," agreed Domi. "She now has a tale to tell."

"Oh," said Belly. "Just like Noah's dragon tale."

"Yeah, right," said Ariel laughing. "No one's going to believe this one either!"

Everyone laughed.

"I'm sure you want to return to your land," said Queen Ellyn. "Tai, if you will give me my crystal, I will send your new friends back."

"Oh, I forgot. I lost your crystal in the tunnel," Princess Tai moaned.

"Don't you have more crystals?" asked Belinda feeling a prickle of panic.

"Willie, didn't you see something after we pushed that cart over?" asked Noah. He turned to find Willie.

Willie was no longer with the group.

"Where *is* my little brother?" Reggie asked looking around.

"Here he comes," pointed Ari as Willie burst out of the castle waving the blue crystal above his head.

Willie hurried over to Queen Ellyn and handed her the black ribbon with the crystal hanging from it.

"Thank you," exclaimed Tai hugging him.

"Don't you think you could have gotten this sooner?" complained Reggie.

"You're just jealous because she hugged me and not you."

Reggie smacked the back of Willie's head. Willie reached out to smack Reggie's head but Noah held his arm.

"Guys … can we get on with this?"

Queen Ellyn tied the black ribbon around her neck. The crystal glowed bright blue as she placed her fingers gently around it. A blue tornado of bright light sizzled and swirled across the bridge and settled in front of them. A huge black hole opened up.

"Wow," said Belly.

"I told you I needed lessons with the crystal," laughed Tai. "I will miss you all," she said hugging each in turn.

Reggie blushed. "Will I see you ever again?" he asked.

"You never know," smiled Tai.

Reggie sighed. "You really are beautiful."

The king frowned at Reggie the Rhino.

"Just saying," he said blushing again.

The girls said good-bye to Princess Tai. They turned and walked into the giant black wormhole together with Willie and Reggie.

"Wait, Noah," called King Merek.

He spoke to his queen, then walked over to Noah and handed him five gold coins stamped with his own likeness.

"Let these Windom coins be medals of honor for the five heroes who saved our castle," he said.

Noah thanked the king. He put the special coins in his pocket, gave a quick salute and followed his friends home.

Chapter 25

"Noah. Noah, wake up."

Noah heard his mother's voice as though she were very far away. He opened his eyes slowly. The school nurse shined a small beam from a flashlight in his eyes to check the size of his pupils.

"What happened?" he asked.

"You tripped coming off the steps and knocked yourself out," answered his mom.

"Again," said his dad. He kneeled on the floor next to the nurse.

"Where's Ariel?" Noah asked. He tried to sit up. He felt like his head would explode. The nurse gently pushed him back down.

"Don't try to get up. The ambulance is on its way."

"Ambulance?"

"Yes, we don't want to move you. The paramedics will take you out on a stretcher."

"It's just a precaution, son," assured his father. "You might have a mild concussion. We want a doctor to check you out."

"Where's Ari?"

"I'm right here," answered his sister standing behind her father. She still held the coin in her fingers.

"How about Belinda, and Willie, and Reggie? Are they alright?"

"Everyone is fine," said Noah's mom. "You are the only one who fell."

"No. I mean did everyone get back from Windom?"

"Not again," said Dad. "Son. No one left the auditorium. We have all been here the whole time you were knocked out."

"But…"

"No buts. Be still and relax."

Noah closed his eyes. *This can't be happening again*, he thought. *Everything had seemed so real. The medals!*

Noah reached into his pocket. His hand closed over the five gold coins.

A shadow passed over his eyelids. Noah looked up and saw Uncle Willard standing over him.

"Please," Noah begged. "I need to know what's real."

Willard smiled and winked. "Yes, I think it's time. Call me when you are home and well again."

Then Willard, the Wise Wizard of Windom, turned and vanished from the auditorium with his two wizard-in-training nephews.

About the Author

JoAnn Flammer is a freelance writer and a retired elementary teacher. She is living 'happily ever after' on Schroon Lake in Adirondack, New York, with her husband, Lee.

JoAnn would love to hear from you. E-mail her at joannflammer@aol.com with the title of the book in the subject line or visit her at joannflammer.com.

Other Books by JoAnn:
The Last Wish for children 8-12 years of age
Giving Your Child an Edge: A Parenting Handbook